Critter Clatter

Rhymes and
Chatter

...

Critter Clatter
Rhymes and Chatter

Carol Schaefer
Boise, Idaho

To my children who inspired me
and to their children who required me
to never lose touch with the beauty and honesty
of a child's mind.

Critter Clatter
Rhymes and
Chatter

Edited by Patricia Entwistle, Boise, Idaho.

Book design and typography by Meggan Laxalt Mackey, Studio M Publications & Design, Boise, Idaho.

Library of Congress Cataloging-in-Publication Data
Schaefer, Carol, 1934 —.
    Critter Clatter: Rhymes and Chatter

Summary:
Critter Clatter: Rhymes and Chatter by author Carol Schaefer is a collection of poems and verses to entertain children and the adults who read with them. It is a fun-filled book of rhymes that will quickly catch and inspire a child's imagination. The author skillfully draws you into the escapades of all kinds of critters, including frogs, a duck, a cow, a pair of goats, an owl, and even a flower that will capture your heart. She has also tucked in some subtle life lessons along the way. Enchanting colorful illustrations by Erin Ann Jensen make the characters come to life while clever words simply dance off the page. It is best read aloud while wearing jammies and robes and curled up together on a soft, comfy sofa.

Published by
Carol Schaefer
ISBN 978-1-0878-9983-1

FIRST PRINTING 2020
IN THE UNITED STATES OF AMERICA

Verses in this Book

Verses in this Book

Rhyming

Oh silly you and silly me,
We are as silly as people can be.
But I don't care—I have a good time.
I like to be silly and make things rhyme.
Rhyming is really quite easy to do.
I rhyme all the time, how about you?

Animal Zoo

I found a place down by the sea—
A little white cottage, just right for me.
I was so happy to move down there,
To walk in the sand in the fresh salty air.
So I packed my things and left straightaway
To the seashore I headed that very same day.

I arrived about a quarter past four,
Put my key in the lock and opened the door.
I heard some noise, a rattling sound.
Someone was in there, stirring around.
Imagine my shock when I saw what was there;
It was enough to really straighten my hair.

In my own little kitchen, busy cooking a meal
Was a big old furry, shiny brown seal.
He waddled around, so silly and fat,
Wearing an apron and a floppy white hat.
He'd made noodles and fish and peas and beans
And an odd-looking dish of sea weedy things.

Next to the fire in my new easy chair
Snoozed a little round, fluffy koala bear.
Perched in my rocker, a big gray cat
Was knitting a sweater, or something like that.

A silly old pelican sat at her feet,
Holding her yarn in his big, roomy beak.
"You've had a long drive; go hop in the shower.
Dinner will be served in just half an hour."

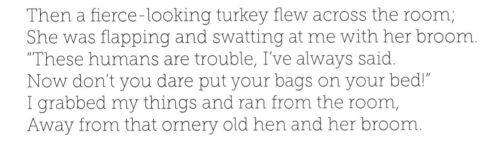

This couldn't be true, it just couldn't be—
The cooking seal was speaking to me!
An old yellow dog stood up with a yawn,
"That's just enough time to mow the lawn."

Then a fierce-looking turkey flew across the room;
She was flapping and swatting at me with her broom.
"These humans are trouble, I've always said.
Now don't you dare put your bags on your bed!"
I grabbed my things and ran from the room,
Away from that ornery old hen and her broom.

In a cozy room with a bed and a chair,
A little white poodle was brushing her hair.
She smiled and nodded at a chest of drawers.
"Put your things in there. This room is yours."
Then, giving the dresser a fond little rub,
She said, "Tell the otter you'll be needing the tub."

I had to sit down; I thought I might faint
When a goat passed my window with a big can of paint.
He was wearing white coveralls and a cap on his head.
This was all too much; I fell on the bed.
Then in flew the turkey, as mad as before.
I rolled off the bed and fell on the floor.
"Just as I thought, you've wrinkled the bed.
I just got finished changing that spread!"

She scared me silly; I shook like a coward,
So I grabbed my things and ran for the shower.
"I do the laundry," said a brown kangaroo.
Drop your clothes in my pouch, and I'll do them up too."

Oh dear, I thought, what a crazy place,
As I scrubbed my head and washed my face.
I combed my hair and put on clean sox;
That's when I met the little red fox.
"I've shined your shoes and pressed your pants.
Now if you'd like, I'll teach you to dance.
The foxtrot, of course, is my favorite one.
Now, pay attention and learn how it's done."

Oh me, oh my, oh mercy sakes.
What was this strange and crazy place?
I had bought this place for peace and a view,
But now I feel like I'm in a zoo!

The scraping of chairs, the rattle of plates
Made me run downstairs, for I dared not be late.
All of the animals were gathered around;
It was suddenly quiet, not one made a sound.
I hurried over and took a chair.
Glancing around, I tried not to stare.
One of them started to say the grace.
It was the goat, with paint on his face.

"Thank you for this food we eat.
Thank you for this home so neat.
We work to keep it clean and nice,
And thank you, Lord, that we have no mice.

"The beds are made, the lawn is mowed.
The laundry's done, the garden's sowed.
The paint is fresh, the food is good.
We've even cut our winter's wood.

"We thank you for the sandy beach,
And thank you for the sea.
We thank you for this real live boy.
He looks just fine to me.

"We're very different, each of us,
But we get along without much fuss.
And one more thing, oh God we pray—
We hope this boy will let us stay."
So, there it is; I can't explain.
But, you know, I let them all remain—
Even the turkey with her awful broom.
The house is small, but there's always room.

So whenever you happen to be down by the sea,
Please stop to visit the animals and me.
The seal will bake cookies and cakes and pies,
And the koala might even open his eyes.

Alligator Day

Yesterday I saw a frog
Who got so mad he kicked a log.
Well, that looked pretty silly to me.
He looked even sillier when he kicked a tree.
I don't know why he was so mad; I didn't wait to see.
I certainly wasn't about to let that frog take a kick at me!

So I slipped past him and went on my way,
Enjoying that beautiful summer day.
I was kicking along an old dirt road
When I came upon a strange old toad.
This toad was blue and rather thin,
And he had whiskers on his chin.
On his head was an old straw hat,
And he swung at me with a baseball bat!

I stopped in my tracks, just looking at him.
He stuck out his tongue and glared and looked grim.
"Why are you standing there looking at me?
How rude, how crude can one boy be?
Have you never seen a toad at all?"
"N—no sir, I've never seen a toad so tall.
I mean I've never seen a toad that's blue.
I've just never seen a toad like you!
I've never seen whiskers on a toad.
Does that mean you're very old?

20

"I never knew a toad could talk or swing a bat ..."
"So, what's so strange about all of that?"
"Well you *do* have whiskers on your chin
And you're so blue and tall and thin.
And...and why do you carry that baseball bat?"
"So I can give noseys like you a whack!
I am what I am, and of course I can talk,
So I can tell you to take a walk!"

He jumped up and down, he'd whack and he'd shout.
He didn't like me, there was simply no doubt.
So, when he kept yelling and batting at me,
I knew it was time for me to flee.
How odd, how strange, how very weird—
A log-kicking frog and a toad with a beard!
I decided to go off a different way;
Too much was happening to me today.

I crossed the road and went down by the river,
Where I tripped over something that still makes me shiver.
There lay a gator, as big as a log,
Big enough to eat me and that toad and that frog!
He wore a polka-dot vest, had a flower in his teeth.
He was grinning at me ... OH GOOD GRAVY, GOOD GRIEF!
To make matters worse, he wore a long wig.
Then that monster got up and started dancing a jig.

A red kerchief was tied in a bow on his tail;
He waved it about and started to wail:
"Skippity-doo-dah, skippity-A,
My oh my, what a fine gator day!"

I started walking backwards, as quiet as could be,
But he stopped his singing and shouted at me.
"Stop right there, boy; You hear what I say?
How dare you come here on Alligator Day?
I'm King of the Gators, Old Gray Head's my name.
Grinning and leering and scaring's my game.
You hear what I say, boy? You listen to me.
You mess with Old Gray Head and you cease to be!
You see this crown upon my head?
You mess with The King, and you wind up dead!"

Well, there *was* no crown—not like the toad with the hat,
But I wasn't gonna tell Old Gray Head that!
If he wore a crown that I couldn't see,
If he thought he was king, that was okay with me.
Just let him keep dancing and singing his song.
This kid was leaving; this kid was gone!

So, while Old Gray Head was busy grooving,
This kid was trucking; this kid was moving.
I went flying back the way I'd come.
You'd better believe that this kid can run!

I got whacked by the toad as I tore on by,
But I never slowed down or batted an eye.
I dashed by the frog, still kicking at trees;
He turned and kicked the back of my knees.
He chased after me a good mile and a half.
I supposed we looked funny, but I couldn't laugh.

"Oh weird, oh strange," I'd groan and moan.
"That's it, I've had it, this kid's going home!"
I thought I might faint any minute from fright.
I wanted my house to come into sight.
And then, there it was, right up ahead—
My house and my mom and my own little bed.

I ran up the stairs, taking two at a time.
I bellowed and howled and whimpered and whined.
"Quick, close the curtains, please lock the door.
This kid's not going out there any more!"

The Owl in the Tree

There's a big fluffy owl who lives in a tree.
He's been such a wonderful friend to me.
He isn't too pretty, not playful at all.
He's just a funny old, fussy old, feathery fowl.
The first time I saw him, so proper and prim,
I simply could not help laughing at him.
But he didn't seem to mind that at all.
Not this funny old, fluffy old, serious owl.

So I sat right down and began to chat,
And he really seemed to enjoy that.
Well, it wasn't long before I could see
That he was an expert at listening to me.

Now I visit that owl almost every day,
And he listens to anything I have to say.
He settles his feathers on a limb of the tree
And just sits there winking and blinking at me.
He never expects me to hush my noise
Or to run and play with the other boys.
Not once has he told me to stop my chatter
Or to go somewhere else with all of my clatter.

I can tell him my troubles, each worry and woe,
And his big eyes answer, "I know, I know."

Whenever I share some nice surprise,
He stares at me and blinks his eyes.
Then he cocks his head, as if to say,
"That's the best surprise I've heard all day!"
When I have a secret that I want him to keep,
My good, feathered friend won't utter a peep.

Of course, he speaks to me once in a while,
But only in his own, very special owl style.
If I say that someone was absent from school,
He fluffs his wings and asks me, "Who?"
If I say that friends are coming to play,
He just wonders "Who?" in his curious way.
If I said that an owl was my best friend,
His ear would flick and his toes would bend.
Then I know exactly what he would do.
He would just look down and holler, "W H O O?"

I think that everyone needs to be heard,
And that's why I like that nice old bird.
He will always be so very special to me,
That funny old, stuffy old owl in the tree.

That Goat in My Boat

One day in my boat, I found a goat.
I asked that goat why he sat in my boat.
"Without a boat I could not float;
That's why this goat is in your boat!"

"You didn't ask permission to sit in my boat."
"I never ask permission," sniffed that sassy goat.
"But you should do what's right, you know."
"I won't discuss it; I have to go!"

"Well, this looks very strange to me,
And, goat, this boat belongs to ME!
Just why do you think you need to float?
Where do you plan to go with my boat?"
"Oh, here or there. I just don't care;
A goat in a boat could go anywhere."

What could I do; what could I say?
How could I get him to go away?
I knew I had to think smarter than him:
"Hey, goat! Why don't you go for a swim?"

"Because I want to stay alive!
I cannot swim; I cannot dive.
Don't bother me—just go away.
You can use your boat another day."
"If you'd come out, we could go for a walk.
We could stroll on the beach and have a nice talk."
"You don't fool me, I won't go walking.
And get this straight, GOATS DON'T LIKE TALKING!
Now, turn around and go back home.
This goat just wants to be alone."

So away he rowed, that crazy goat.
He rowed away like he owned my boat.
Oh me, oh my! What would YOU do
If a crazy goat stole your boat from you?

I watched him go a-rowing.
Wherever was he going?
I watched him row clear out of sight.
I watched for that goat all day and night.
I sat and waited on the shore
Until I was tired and stiff and sore.

I've never again seen that terrible goat,
And I've never again seen my own little boat.
Now every time I meet a goat
I wonder if HE stole my boat.
I think that I shall never know
Where that goat in my boat was determined to go.

A Flower Named George

My name is George, and I'm proud of my name.
There are a great many Georges, but we're not all the same.
I've been told I look strange, but I don't really care;
It's being so different that makes me so rare.

The first time I opened my face to the sun,
The flowers all laughed, "Look at this one!
He's different, he's different, as different can be.
Why, he's not at all like you and like me!

"His stem is silver, and his leaves are yellow.
I say, he's a very strange little fellow.
His petals are orange, purple, red, blue, and green.
He's different, he's different, you see what I mean?"

"He's not a pansy, a violet or rose.
What is he, what is he, what do you suppose?"
"He's not a bluebell or a dainty sweet pea.
He's surely no hollyhock; what can he be?"

"I know he's no daisy! Of course he's no mum!
He's not a petunia! I think he looks dumb!"
"Whoever saw such a flower as he?
What can he, what can he, what can he be?"

"Could he be an iris or maybe a carnation?
What IS he, what IS he, WHAT IN TARNATION?"
"He's not on a bush!" "Well, he's not on a tree!"
"We don't like him; he's different—not like you and me."

Oh, I felt so bad, I wanted to die.
I hid in my leaves, and I started to cry.

"Please don't mock me and keep me apart.
This is so upsetting, it hurts my heart.
I'm God's funny rainbow on a stem, don't you see?
It just makes me wilt when you make fun of me.
Just being different does not make me bad,
And my being different should not make you mad.

"God didn't think we should all be the same,
So he made me different, with a different kind of name.
God put me together right there on his knee,
Then he laughed and he laughed with heavenly glee.
He rumbled and shook with a great mighty sound
Until I bounced off and stuck in the ground."

Then God knitted his brow and thought for a while.

"By George, you are different, the most different yet.
But different's not easy; they'll tease you, I'll bet."

29

"Your life won't be easy if they turn you away,
But, George, you listen to what I have to say.
Don't ever worry, and please don't feel blue.
If the flowers love me, they will learn to love you."

I tried to be brave, but my eyes got all teary.
Tears splashed on my petals and got them all smeary.

"LISTEN MY CHILDREN" said a voice from above—
A voice that sounded like a river of love.
"Oh, stop, my lovelies; stop right away!
Be very careful of the things you say.
Think, little ones; what are you doing—
Jeering and sneering, sniffing and booing?
Poor little George. When you make fun of him,
I can see his beautiful spirit dim.
Never, ever dim another one's light!
Think, my children, and do what's right."

Well, I must have looked like a strange, funny, sight.
The flowers clapped their leaves and laughed in delight.

"You're so shiny, you sparkle, you're bright as the sun.
Oh stay with us, George; we think you are fun."

I felt so happy as I dried my eyes,
I looked at my petals and got a surprise—
My tears made them shiny, so shiny and bright,
I was all lit up with a heavenly light.

"We're sorry, George. We love you and your name.
You've made us so happy that we're not all the same."

Wouldn't this world be a dreary old place
If everyone in it had the same kind of face?
If everyone thought and acted like me,
There would never be anything different to see.
If we all did everything just like you,
There would never be anything different to do.

So, whenever you meet someone different from you,
Remember the flowers and George and what love can do.

31

Nanny and Billy

There is something funny about a goat,
With his silly beard and shaggy coat.
Have you seen the gleam in his shiny black eyes?
He's such a "mischief"—so full of surprise.

Our dad says a goat always spells trouble;
And when you have two, your trouble is double!
But Mother thought goat milk was good for us,
So our dad gave in without much fuss.

We have a pasture near our backdoor,
With room for two goats and many more.
"All right," said our dad; "One goat or two.
But keep them out of my store, whatever you do!"

We didn't think it would be too hard
To keep two goats in such a big yard.
So off we went to visit the farmers.
We found two goats, and they were charmers.
One was black, and the other was white.
They were so lively, funny, and bright.

"What sweet little goats you have in there;
We would like very much to buy this pair.

"We hope you don't want a great deal of money."
Somehow, the farmer thought that was too funny.
He laughed so hard and slapped his knee;
Why, I've never seen such outright glee.
He said, "Young lady, buy one from me,
And I'll gladly throw in that second one free."

So he tied them up in the back of our truck;
Then he smiled and waved and wished us good luck.
We drove home as happy as we could be—
We had only bought one goat; the other was free.

We called one Nanny and the other one Billy.
They were so cute, so naughty and silly.
They kicked and b-a-a-a-ed and made such a fuss,
I don't think those goats were too happy with us.

Nanny ate the ribbon Betty wore on her curls,
And Billy broke the string that held Mother's pearls.
It was hard to be mad at this funny pair;
You couldn't help laughing at their beady-eyed stare.

We put them out back while we ate our lunch,
And had nearly finished when we heard a big CRUNCH!
Our dad jumped up and ran to see.
He was followed by Mother, Betty, and me.
There on the back porch, in a whole case of eggs,
Stood two, four, six—eight hairy legs.
Oh my, what a terrible mess we had!
And such a waste—our mother was mad.

She lifted her broom, and it came down ker-splat
Right on Billy's black hairy back!
She waved that broom at Nanny too.
"What a terrible thing for you goats to do!"
That pair went running out into the pasture,
With mother behind, running even faster.

The next day started out all right
Until Nanny and Billy got into a fight.
I tied them to the clothesline poles,
But that didn't help, because bless their souls,
They found Mother's wash hanging out in the sun
And decided a tug-of-war would be fun.
Billy pulled one way and Nanny the other.
You should have seen our poor tired mother.
She went dashing out again with her broom
And whacked at those goats—kaboom! kaboom!

"Oh dear," she sighed, "what will we do,
If those goats of ours continue to chew?
They've torn sheets and towels and socks red and blue,
And now they've chewed your dad's trousers too."

The next day, Mother planned a surprise;
She had baked three nice fluffy lemon pies.
But when we found the pies, we hid our eyes;
Goats in our pies really were a surprise!
Mother said she thought she had made a mistake;
It seemed now that she could not even bake.

Dad said, "I knew there'd be trouble with those pets.
I was afraid you'd eventually have some regrets.
I know you thought two goats would be nice,
But you should have taken my good advice.
You simply must teach your goats to be good
And behave the way two nice pets should."

While our mother and father were busy talking,
Our naughty pets had gone a-walking.
They got in our dad's store before we knew it,
And we had promised *never* to let them do it.

If there's anything worse than two goats in a store,
The only thing worse, I suppose, would be more.
They pulled at our dad's big ball of string,
And wrapped it and wound it around everything.

They chewed on boxes and balanced on pails,
And scattered the candy, the gum, and the nails.
Billy turned the flour barrel upside down.
It dusted him white—he looked like a clown.
They spilled all the sugar, the rice, and the oats.
A cyclone could be no worse than those goats.
Our dad kept pickles in a big wooden keg;
Nanny stirred them around with her right front leg.
The keg tipped over and she fell out,
And slipped and tumbled and splashed about.
Our father ran in, but she slid right past;
Then Billy decided to get out of there fast.

They seemed to be saying, "We're sorry, sir;
We didn't mean to cause such a stir."
Not even our dad could stay mad at them.
"C'mon goats, we'll try again."

Well, things were quiet for a little while,
But quiet isn't a healthy goat's style.
So, as you might know, one summer's day,
When Charlie Smith drove out our way,
In his big new car with a canvas top,
Some trouble was almost sure to pop.

We paid no attention—that car was so grand—
To the fact that our Billy was near at hand.
He started to run and then to jump—
On top of that car, he lit with a thump!

I couldn't look, did not want to see.
Charlie's wife started yelling, "Heaven help me!
That crazy goat just jumped through our top.
I told you, Charlie, I said not to stop!"
Billy's sharp little feet cut right through that top.
His legs went through before he could stop.
When Dad came out, he could only stare.
I think he was ready to pull his hair.

"Mother," he called, "Come out here right now!
If you really want milk, please just buy a cow!
I simply will not keep this pair about.
They'll have to leave; *they must get out*!"

Both Nanny and Billy looked very sad;
I don't really think they meant to be bad.
"Oh, don't make them go," we started to tease.
"We will keep them penned up—please, Father, please!"
We begged our father most of that day,
Until he decided that our goats could stay.

Nanny and Billy are still living with us,
And now and again, they still cause a fuss.
But now those two have a cute little kid,
And three cause more trouble than two ever did.

Yes, our funny goats are still about,
Even though sometimes they make our dad shout.
And sometimes they make our poor mother run,
But we love our pets—they are such fun!

Tuck the Duck

There was a duck;
His name was Tuck.
Tuck did not like to swim around;
He felt much better on the ground.
Tuck didn't even like to fly,
He felt so silly in the sky.
Tuck thought that it was just bad luck
That he was born to be a duck.

This Tuck would rather be a boy.
Boys always seemed so full of joy.
Tuck liked to watch them in their play;
He even cried when they went away.
He liked the way they wore their hats
And played around with balls and bats.
He liked to see them dig in their jeans
For string and rocks and jellybeans.

Tuck liked the noises they could make;
And he loved their mothers' chocolate cake.
They made big bubbles with their gum;
They played with tops that spin and hum.
He liked it when they shouted and yelled.
He even liked the way they smelled—
Like dusty worms and peppermint kisses,
So full of fun and dreams and wishes.

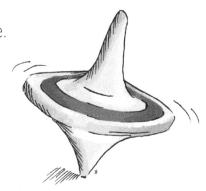

But most of all, he liked their shoes.
A duck with shoes, wouldn't *that* be news?
Shoes seemed to be such magic things.
He liked them better than his old wings.
They kick and skip and jump so high,
A duck with shoes wouldn't need to fly.

If only he had a bright red pair,
He'd be a duck beyond compare.
Where did they find such magic things,
With soft white soles and tangled strings?

So he followed a boy away from the pond
And waddled into the world beyond.
While the boy went into a candy store,
Tuck waited outside the big glass door.
The boy came out with candy on a stick,
Which he began to suck and lick.

No, the magic shoes were not in there.
Where, Tuck wondered, could he find a pair?
Then Tuck saw a wonderful sight—
There in a window, so colorful and bright,
He saw those shoes, shoes by the dozens,
Enough for Tuck and all his cousins.
He went right through the open door
And quacked and waddled around the floor.

The man in the store tried to shoo him away,
But Tuck wouldn't leave, he was going to stay.
Tuck *had* to make the man understand,
So he reached up and took his hand.
He led the man past a table of socks,
Up to the shoes in the window box.

"Oh my," said the man. "You don't want those.
They're much too small; they'll pinch your toes.
Ducks just *never* wear shoes, you know,
And you have no money, so you must go!"

But Tuck had found a big red pair
And was pulling them on with loving care.
So the big man laughed and said, "Alright,"
And watched Tuck waddle out of sight.

Now things are quite different for Mr. Tuck,
But in spite of the shoes, he *is* still a duck.
Ever since Tuck made his dream come true,
He doesn't do things that other ducks do.
Instead, he skips and jumps and kicks.
He's not too nice—he bites and picks.

Well, shoes are fine for folks like us,
But shoes on a duck cause a terrible fuss.
What will Tuck do when his shoes wear out?
I suppose he'll just sit around and pout.

There's a Hole in My Ceiling

There's a hole in my ceiling—I don't know why.
I look at the ceiling and see the sky.
The sun shines in; the moon does too.
The rain falls down, and the wind blows through.

What made that hole,
I'm sure I don't *know*.
Where did it come from?
Where did it go?
Where's the piece that used to be?
Where's the piece I can no longer see?

If it fell down, it would be on the floor;
It certainly didn't just walk out the door.
I know I should fix it, but I don't know how.
Perhaps I'll go out and ask that cow.

"There's a hole in my ceiling. Where did it go?"
"What makes you think a cow would know?"
"I thought you could tell me what to do."
"*Well,*" said the cow, "If I were *you* ..."

She thought a bit as she chewed her cud,
"I think I'd stuff that hole with mud."
"But how would I get the mud to stay?
The rain would wash it all away."

"Well, why did you ask me anyhow?
For heaven's sake, I'm just a cow.
Don't ask a cow a thing like that.
You'd do much better to ask the cat.
Of course, she never tells the truth,
But I know that cat's been on your roof.
She was up there scratching, meowing, and hissing.
I'll bet she took the part that's missing."
What an ornery thing for that cow to say;
Then she waved her tail and walked away.
Why would the cat do a thing like that?
She blamed that hole on a poor little cat!

Then I thought to myself, oh yes, of course;
I'll go to the stables and ask the horse.
"There's a hole in my ceiling. What shall I do?"
"Well, son, I think if I were you,
I'd stuff that hole up there with hay."
"But I worry the hay would blow away."
"So why ask me? What do I know?
I'm just a horse. I can't even sew."
"No one can sew up holes in ceilings."
"Well, now you've gone and hurt my feelings!"
"There's a piece of the roof up there that's gone.
It's not in the house, and it's not on the lawn."
"I'd look in the barn or someplace like that.
If I were you, I'd ask that darn cat!"

That horse was pretty ornery too,
So I called the dog and asked what he'd do.
"I'd bury that hole deep in the ground.
It works quite well for bones, I've found."
"Bury a hole in a hole, you say?
Whatever makes you think that way?"
"Because I dig holes and cover them over.
What do you expect from a guy named Rover?
Why did you ask me a thing like that?
If you want to know, go ask the cat."

Then, over my head, a bird flew by.
He turned and looked me right in the eye.
"There's a hole in your ceiling; I don't know why.
I see a lot when I'm high in the sky.
I'd stuff that hole with twigs and fluff.
Birds are quite good at fixing stuff.
But I've seen that cat go sneaking around
Up on your roof and all over the ground.
Believe me, you can take my word,
That cat's no friend to mouse or bird."
Before I could think of a thing to say,
That bird took off and flew away.

Well, the time had come to talk to the cat.
"There's a hole in my ceiling. Do you know about that?"
"Of course I do, I've known all along.
There's a hole in your roof; some of it's gone.

"I'd call a roofer if I were you.
Any cat knows that's the thing to do."
So the roofer came with a big tall ladder.
He climbed on my roof to see what was the matter.
"There's a hole in your roof and your ceiling too.
It's a good thing you called; I can fix it for you.
Some shingles are missing; they've just blown away.
Don't worry about it. I'll fix it today."

The shingles blew off, it's as simple as that.
And everyone blamed that hole on the cat!

The Cow Who Couldn't Moo

The silliest thing I ever knew
Was a poor little cow who couldn't moo.
I'm sorry to say she did not know how;
Nothing she did made her sound like a cow.
Her mother said, "Dear, you mustn't worry,
And you shouldn't be in such a hurry.
Mooing is something all cows do.
I just never knew one to worry like you."
Then her mother turned and went away
To chew her cud and to munch some hay.

But the poor little cow didn't feel much better.
She wouldn't even let the children pet her.
How unhappy she was, so worried and blue;
Still she found such comical things to do.
One day she hid in a clump of trees,
And there she took lessons from the bees.
When she came out, she could buzz just fine.
She could buzz and whirr and even whine.
But that isn't how a cow should sound,
And she stopped when she saw how the other cows frowned.

Then she found a ball of shiny black fur;
That was the cat who taught her to purr.
Now, a well-learned purr does not make one a cat;
Still, she was meowing and scratching, and things like that.

She licked her hoof to wash her face
But fell down and sprawled all over the place.
She kept right on trying in spite of her fall,
In hopes of becoming a cat after all.
Then a dog heard her purr and started to chase.
You could see the surprise all over her face.
Nobody wants to be chased like that,
So she gave up trying to be a cat.

No, a purring cow would just never do.
So she called on a dove who taught her to coo.
The cooing, she found, was really quite easy,
But somehow it made her feel very sneezy.

She forgot about cooing and went on her way,
And then met a donkey who taught her to bray.
But braying was hard, and it made her so weary;
And, anyway, braying didn't sound very cheery.

She asked a fat pig to teach her to squeal,
But he was too busy eating his meal.
She practiced crowing with a fine old cock,
And thought she had really learned how to squawk;
But when she perched on the fence at dawn,
She couldn't crow, she could only yawn.

The turkey said, "You should try to gobble,"
But her gobble came out with a terrible wobble.
On her way to the pond to visit the duck,
She met a red hen and learned how to cluck.

But clucking, of course, is not for a cow,
So she called to a horse who was pulling a plow.
Of course, he said, he could teach her to neigh,
But he didn't like cows who talked that way.

As she sadly walked on to find the duck,
She had what you might call a bit of bad luck.
The ground by the pond was not very firm,
And soon she was stuck too tight to squirm.

Now she was in a terrible spot.
She was tired and thirsty and frightened and hot.
She needed to moo so badly now;
She just had to sound like a regular cow.
If she didn't moo, it would soon be too late;
But all she could do was imitate.

Too impatient to learn a sound of her own,
She had copied everything from a dove to a drone.
So she made no sound of any kind—
No cluck, no purr, no bark or whine.
She shed a very big cow-sized tear;
She was worried and sad and full of fear.

Then above her ear flew a wee little flea.
This flea was feeling as mean as could be.
He saw the cow and zoomed in near
And bit her hard right on the ear.
Well, to bite that poor cow was a mean thing to do,
And without thinking at all, she let out a big MOO!

"Oh, I do have a moo—it was there all along!
I was too worried, impatient, and wrong."
She kept on mooing so she'd remember how,
And soon she was rescued by the farmer and his plow.

"Little cow, you sounded a good alarm.
Why, you have the best moo on the farm!"
She was muddy but proud, as he scratched her ear.
She winked her big eyes to hide a tear.
And she knew she'd be patient forevermore.
She had learned that good things are worth waiting for.

Grandma's Bed

Sometimes in early morning,
I will climb in Grandma's bed
And pull all Grandma's covers
Clear up and over my head.

And when she comes into the room,
She pretends that I'm not there.
She sets about to make the bed,
With very special care.

"I've never seen such a lumpy bed.
Whatever can it be?
And then she thumps and plumps until
I yell, "Hey Gram that lump is me."

So then she grabs her pillow
And really tosses it about.
And I duck and laugh and holler
Until she rolls me out.

Little Bits: Short Verses

Billy Biggs
Billy Biggs takes care of pigs,
But pigs don't like this Billy Biggs.
When Billy's around, the pigs get thin;
All of their food goes into him!

A Hole in the Ground
I looked into a hole in the ground,
And what do you suppose I found?
Well, you should know as well as me,
The hole was dark, I could not see.

Sad Old Witch
One day I met a sad old witch;
She was sitting beside a narrow ditch.
There by her side was a wooden broom.
She wanted to swim, but there wasn't room
In the ditch
For a broom and a witch.

My Socks
Oh stop! Don't walk! I cannot go.
My shoe, you see, it hurts my toe.
But then perhaps it's just my socks.
My socks, you see, are full of rocks.

The Groundhog

Said Charlie Ray on Groundhog Day:
Will winter stay or go away?
I suppose I should be stirring about.
I should go to the hole and stick my head out.

I'm supposed to see if my shadow's out there,
But between you and me, I don't really care;
Because, you see, if I had my choosing,
I'd just roll over and go right on snoozing.

But human beings for their own silly reasons
Depend upon me to predict the seasons.
I don't understand how humans think,
But I'll stick out my head and peek and blink.
After spending the winter in this dark, black hole,
The sun hurts my eyes, I suppose you know.

If my shadow is out there lurking about,
I'll come back inside and not go out.
That means that I can go back to bed;
Six weeks of winter are still ahead.

But if my shadow is nowhere in sight,
The humans will dance around in delight.
Because winter is over and spring is ahead,
Then I won't be able to go back to bed!

Christmas Tree

I found a pretty Christmas tree.
I think it grew there just for me.
Already trimmed in soft white snow,
I could not cut it; I let it grow.

Special Company

There's someone we expect, you see—
Some very special company.
We won't wait up—that is because
Our special guest is Santa Claus.

It does seem rather strange to me—
Company we never see.
We always try to sneak a peek,
But he never comes till we're asleep.

My Dog

I taught my dog to sit and beg.
I taught him to stand on one front leg.
I taught him to roll over and play dead.
I even taught him to stand on his head.
But I did not teach him to chase that cat.
I certainly did not teach him that.

My Kite

I sailed my kite away up high
Into an icy blue March sky.
I wanted to climb right up its tail;
Then, away my kite and I would sail.

And when the string was dropped down there,
We'd sail even higher into the air.
And then, you know, in the blink of an eye,
We'd just disappear; away we'd fly.

We'd float so high, we'd float so far,
I'd bump my head upon a star.
And then we'd drift back to the ground,
Just whisper down without a sound.

The Fizz

Well, I have something different to see;
I have no idea what it could be.
It's so very strange, no one knows what it is,
But it says a Fizz is what it is.
I asked it, "Just what is a Fizz?"
"A Fizz, that's what this big Fizz is."
"But you're such a puzzlement to me,
I just don't know what a Fizz could be."
"I SAID A FIZZ IS WHAT IT IS."
So, here it is, a big old Fizz.
But I know one thing about that Fizz—
A big old grump is what it is.

Fish

I caught a fish with bright green hair.
Well, a fish with hair is quite a scare.
I didn't keep him; I threw him back
And caught another whose hair was black
Should I keep this one or throw him back too?
If I caught another, his hair might be blue.
I wish you'd tell me what to do.
I don't want a fish whose hair is blue.

Dickie Gandy

Dickie Gandy is a dandy;
He lives on sodas and sugar candy.
He will not eat at suppertime,
And he thinks drinking milk is just a crime.
Someday when he opens his mouth to shout,
He'll get a surprise—his teeth will fall out.

Wair

I once knew a fellow by the name of Wair.
Wair was always trying to grow some hair.
Wair never had a hair on his head;
It grew all over his feet instead.

Why?

Why does an elephant eat with his nose,
And why do monkeys swing by their toes?
Why is that thing on your head called a hat?
I always wonder about things like that.
Who gave the rhinoceros such a big name?
If his name was Mike, would he still be the same?
Why do ladies like to paint their toes,
And why did that fly choose to land on my nose?
Why do dogs like to say bow-wow,
While kittens prefer to say meow?
I wonder if grownups remember at all
What it's like to be only three feet tall,
When chairs are so high you can't reach the floor—
Do you think they remember those things anymore?
I wonder why I always ask why.
I suppose I'm just a curious guy.

Jude

I know a boy, his name is Jude;
But I'm sorry to say he's very rude.
We went on a picnic; I had baked a cake.
Jude threw my cake into the lake.
I offered him a piece of bread.
He set the bread upon his head.
I will not ask him back tonight.
I'll ask a child who is polite.

Things People Say

Have you ever stopped to listen to the things some people say?
I mean, they talk to children in a most peculiar way.
"You've grown another foot, my dear; oh yes, I do declare."
I quickly take a worried peek—there's only two down there.

And, "Isn't it astonishing—why, he's his Uncle Sam."
Well, I don't mean to argue, but I'm myself, I am!
"Well, strike me dead if you don't look exactly like your dad!"
I don't think I look like him; I'm just a little lad.
Now, if I looked just like my dad, then I'd be six feet tall.
My feet would be three times this big, and I'd be slightly bald.

"Oh, what a darling baby! He has his grandpa's nose."
But he wouldn't be so darling if he was wearing one of those.
And I just saw his grandpa; he was here a minute ago.
His nose was still upon his face; I saw it, so I know.

"Oh precious little angel, she has her mother's hair."
Whatever are they saying?—I wonder in despair.
That baby grew her own hair right there upon her head.
Why would she be wearing her mother's hair instead?
Now, that would look completely strange, and I just don't mean maybe.
Her mother's hair is very long; it's longer than the baby.

Old Ron and Me

We dug a fort beneath a tree.
We dug a fort, old Ron and me.
It's up behind our grandpa's home,
Where Ron and I can be all alone.

Up on the hill, beneath a tree,
We dug that fort, old Ron and me.
We worked and worked one summer day—
A perfect place for guys to play.

Oh gosh, that fort of ours is neat.
From there we'd spot the enemy fleet
And send a message to control
That aliens are on patrol.

We'd lie in wait for wagon trains
Or search the sky for enemy planes.
We'd contact folks from outer space,
Old Ron and me in our special place.

A Book

A book is a star that God hung in your night
To fill you with wonder, suspense, and delight.
A book is a spaceship, a rocket to ride.
A book is a warm, faithful dog at your side.

A book lets you dive to the floor of the sea;
It lets you be anything you want to be.
A book is a jet plane that lifts you so high
You're the thunder and lightning that startles the sky.

A book is a helper, a pal, and a friend.
A book is a movie you don't want to end.
A book is a laugh, a giggle, a smile.
A book is a phone you just pick up and dial
To hear voices that speak out of the past
Telling wonderful stories, tales that will last.

A book is that song that goes 'round in your head.
A book is a dream that you watch while in bed.
A book is a key that you must never lose—
A key to all doors, any gateway you choose.

A book is a window that lets in the sun.
A book is a record of all that's been done.
A book is a good time you have by yourself.
A book is adventure waiting there on your shelf.

The Gramatron

Gram calls herself a Gramatron,
With very special powers.
I say, "You're not"; she says, "I am,"
And this goes on for hours.

I say, "You're not a Gramatron,"
Then she gives me her special gaze.
She doesn't spank, she doesn't scold,
She zaps me with Gramatron rays.

I tell her I can't feel them;
Her rays don't hurt a bit.
But that's the thing about Gramatron rays—
You never know when they hit.

But when you're doing something
That you know you shouldn't do,
Quite suddenly the Gramatron rays
Will grab ahold of you.

So, before you do that ornery thing
That you've been planning out,
You'd better stop and think a bit;
There's a Gramatron about.

Acknowledgments

I would especially like to thank my family members, who were the inspiration for many of these verses.

Many thanks to Pat Entwistle who read a couple of my humble hand-written verses, scooped up my whole folder, and ran home to type all of them into legible form. Shortly thereafter, she re-emerged with Meggan Laxalt Mackey of Studio M Publications & Design and Meggan's daughter, Erin Jensen, a talented artist/illustrator, in tow. Wow! I had the A-Team who took *Critter Clatter* out of my closet and brought you this book. I can't thank them enough.

About the Author

Carol Schaefer is a mom, grandma, and great-grandma who has lived her entire life in Idaho and has had many exciting adventures along the way.

These fanciful verses have sprung to life from experiences with her children, their children, and their children over a period of several decades and delighted three generations as they tumbled from her imagination.

Critter Clatter: Rhymes and Chatter is now a collection of Carol's playful yet meaningful words—truly a gift for children of all ages to enjoy.

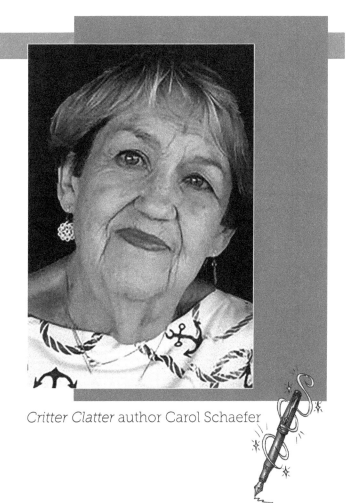

Critter Clatter author Carol Schaefer

CPSIA information can be obtained
at www.ICGtesting.com
Printed in the USA
LVHW022103151020
668892LV00008B/47